Sheeka

by Pratima Mitchell
illustrated by Dave Smith

Contents

PEARSON
Longman

Text © Pratima Mitchell 2003
Series editors: Martin Coles and Christine Hall

PEARSON EDUCATION LIMITED
Edinburgh Gate
Harlow
Essex CM20 2JE
England

www.longman.co.uk

First published 2003
ISBN 0582 79611 3

Illustrated by Dave Smith

Printed in Great Britain by Scotprint, Haddington

This story is dedicated to Hannah and her children.

The publishers' policy is to use paper manufactured from sustainable forests.

Chapter One

Polly
Sunday afternoon, 6th June

This is what happened the night Chrissie ran away.

For Polly it was the most terrifying moment of her life. The atmosphere round the dinner table crackled with electricity. An unbearable silence fell heavily, like a theatre curtain. After that, the scene quickly changed as all hell broke loose.

Dad's mouth set in a thin, disapproving line. "Chrissie, listen to what I have to say," he said in a weary voice to Polly's older sister. "You've got exams next week and from what I can see you're going to fail." His voice rose in anger. "If you think I'm going to support you when you haven't made the slightest effort to work YOU ARE MISTAKEN!" he roared.

Chrissie jumped up, knocking a glass of red

wine and spilling its contents like dark blood on the white cloth. "I'm just sick to death of the lot of you," she screamed, pushing her chair over. She took her dinner plate in both hands and smashed it on the floor. Spaghetti and tomato sauce flew up everywhere.

"Who's going to clean that?" Polly thought, as red streams crawled down the wall.

Chrissie's face was a mask of fury. Eyebrows knitted, eyes flashing, mouth twisted, teeth bared. She looked like someone from a bad Hallowe'en film. Polly had seen the expression before, but then her sister had been acting, flinging herself around the room practising her lines and pausing to read from her script. That was make-believe. This was real. It sent horrid icy fingers snaking down Polly's back.

"I'm going and I'm never coming back. I hate you all and you make me sick to my stomach," Chrissie's voice rang out. Polly couldn't believe that she meant it, but it was hard to read her sister's expression, since Chrissie had left the room dramatically. They heard her going thump, thump, thump up the stairs. A door slammed in the distance.

Just to show whose side she was on, Sheeka got up from her basket by the fire, shook herself daintily and waddled out of the kitchen to haul herself slowly up to Chrissie's room.

* * * * *

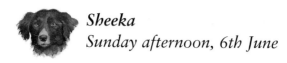

Sheeka
Sunday afternoon, 6th June

I really don't know what to do.

I try everything I can think of to make Chrissie feel better, calmer, more at peace with things. I give her all the love I can to make her feel she's needed. I try to show her how much I adore her. I carry my floppy stuffed rabbit and drop it in her lap, and even offer her my bones. She smiles and hugs me, but then she's off on her restless moods again. Then we walk the streets endlessly; sometimes we get on a train and go to London, or go to visit Dizzy.

Dizzy lives in a strange place with high walls round it. You have to go through a small door, and I get left outside, tied up to a railing. Chrissie is always nervous. I can feel her trembling deep inside.

Her stepmother Emilia tries to help. She always does, but Chrissie never pays any attention to her.

Emilia said, "Chreesie dear, it takes too much time to visit Dizzy in prison. You waste one whole day, and you cannot afford that right now."

"Mind your own business."

"How dare you talk to Emilia like that!" Dad cut in.

That's how the fight had started, the worst fight they'd had.

* * * * *

I nuzzle Chrissie, place my right paw on her foot, but she's too busy pulling clothes, papers, brushes, books out of cupboards and drawers.

"Sheeka, we're going to run away. Right now, this very night. You must be very quiet and good and not give the game away."

Now she's throwing things into a big rucksack. I hope she remembers my dog biscuits. I get quite faint if I don't have a snack every few hours.

She's packed the picture of her mother and the one of me, when I was younger and slimmer, on little three-year-old Polly's lap. This can only mean that we are going somewhere for a long, long time.

I whine quietly, not enough to annoy, but just to show her that it's going to be uncomfortable and inconvenient for an old lady like me. It's cold outside and raining, the thin fine rain that drenches in seconds. "Oh Chrissie," I whine, "can't this running away business wait until the morning?"

We leave and no one stops us. Not even Polly comes running after us. I follow Chrissie, and I recognise where we're going. We're heading for the train station.

* * * * *

Polly
Sunday night, 6th June

All that night Polly tossed and turned. It was impossible to sleep when her sister had left the house in such terrible circumstances and Sheeka was gone too. What would happen now? Was Chrissie spending the night with one of her friends, and would she and Sheeka be back by breakfast? There was no telling with Chrissie. Sometimes she didn't speak to anyone for days. Polly longed for everything to sort itself out as she burrowed under her duvet and tried hard to think of something else.

There was no sign of Chrissie the following morning, or the morning after that. The days turned into weeks and Polly and her parents hoped each day to hear from Chrissie and Sheeka, but there was no word.

Chapter Two

Sheeka
Sunday, 20th June

Chrissie and I have been travelling for a long time now, staying with her friends for a few days and then moving on. Chrissie looks happier than I've seen her for a long time. Maybe because she isn't poring over books. She buries her face in my back and puts her arms round me. "I'm glad I missed my exams. Dad can't make me go to university."

I don't know what university is, but it surely must be an awful place for Chrissie to be so scared of it.

The weather is getting hotter and hotter, and this latest journey we are on seems to take forever. She took out all her savings from the post office today, so it must be all right. Of course it must.

After several train journeys and then some hitch-hiking, we arrive in Glastonbury and make our way to the field which I remember from last year.

I can smell Dog-Dog from far away. My best friend! Dog-Dog's human is a friend of Dizzy's called Id and Id's girlfriend is Scarlett. They are all snug inside a tepee when we finally arrive at the campsite. Fires are smoking everywhere; vapours of meals cooking, damp grass, animals and humans swirl in the evening air and revive me. I start jumping and running around with excitement. The settlement is a muddle of tents, vans, and tepees.

Luckily the rain has cleared and, apart from the mud, it's turned out to be a fine evening.

The humans meet with a lot of hugging and kissing, but Dog-Dog and I have a wrestling match outside the tepee. He tells me the news and I hear that Rhubarb, Custard, Lovelyboy and Crowbar are all here as well to take part in the summer solstice celebrations. What fun we're going to have, all us doggy friends.

"Longest day of the year it is. All them wood spirits'll be out I reckon, and the tree people. They like it when we be fussing and chanting tomorrow. Does honour to their gods, see."

Dog-Dog is a country lad brought up on country lore, so I daren't laugh at him. He takes all this stuff pretty seriously.

"Hey Sheeka, hey Dog-Dog! Sausage!" With yelps of pleasure we leap forward.

Oh, how I love coming to visit Id and Scarlett. They eat sausage and bacon and stews. It does me a power of good to get some meat inside me. Chrissie makes me survive on a vegetarian diet.

Dog-Dog and I are content to sleep outside, because it's now quite warm. The fun is going to begin the next day!

I hate to admit it, but Dog-Dog may be right. There is something special about Glastonbury.

There's the strange, steep hill of the Tor looming above us, and the Abbey and the Holy Well. Dog-Dog told me the humans once had a leader called King Arthur. "Thousands of years ago it was, Sheeka my old pal. This king had a pack, the Knights of the Round Table – anyhow, cutting a long story short, *they* were on the side of good. They fought against evil, and there's magic in the land because this is where they lived. You can feel the magic here, and it draws all these folk to come singing and dancing and be happy."

* * * * *

Sheeka
Monday, 21st June

We're up at dawn to see the sunrise behind the Tor. A procession of humans dressed in long white robes stand in a circle and chant.

Dog-Dog growls, "This is ancient it is – as old as the rocks, as old as the hills and streams. The nature spirits like to hear their prayers."

The humans lift their hands up to the Sun, join them together and bow. Everyone claps and laughs and cheers. Then we all go off to find breakfast.

All over town I trot behind Chrissie and her

pals. The sun warms my back and life feels very good. At lunchtime we picnic on Scotch eggs and bacon butties in the Abbey grounds, then we wander round looking at people throwing pieces of wood in the air and catching them, three or four, one after the other. Oh, how I used to love chasing after sticks when I was young!

There's fun all round. Food stalls with loads of leftovers in bins, music, and all our friends, the other dogs. We all do our silent yaps, which humans can't hear.

"Hey-ho Custard, how's your new pups?"

"Where've you been Lovelyboy? Haven't had sight or sound of you for a year, isn't it?"

"Eeh, Crowbar what's it like in Wales then?"

In the evening the humans make music. It is a full moon and the singing and guitar and drumming go on till the early hours.

Dog-Dog pricks up his ears when a cloud covers the moon. "Hark! Did you hear them?" he says, in a sort of under-growl. I suppose he means the nature spirits. I whine softly and Chrissie puts her arm round me.

"So where are you heading next?" asks one of her friends.

"As far away from my family as possible."

* * * * *

Polly
Monday, 21st June

There had been no news from Chrissie for weeks now. Polly had cautiously checked the bottom drawer of Chrissie's desk where she kept her post office savings book soon after she'd run away. It wasn't there. She knew Chrissie had saved up quite a bit, so at least the two runaways wouldn't starve.

"Really," thought Polly feeling cross, "I wish she'd at least call. She's taken her mobile with her. She must know how worried I am."

Chapter Three

Sheeka
Saturday, 18th September

The more you travel the more you forget. I hardly remember my snug basket by the fire at home. We've been to so many places now and met so many different people. Some of them have smelled really nice and friendly; others have made the hairs on my back stand up. Dog-Dog and I decide that our favourite place has been the seaside – it's so open and so free. We run along the sands chasing one another. Then we splash in the water. When we come out we love to annoy everyone by shaking ourselves near them.

"Where shall we go now, Sheeka?" Chrissie whispers in my ear. We are eating chips on the beach with Scarlett, Id and some of the other regulars. Chrissie pulls on a sweater, which hasn't seen a washing machine for months. Autumn is nearly here.

Dave says, "We're heading for Wales tomorrow. Want a lift to Brecon? It's a really nice camp and you can share our tent. Thing is, we've only room for one in the car. The dogs are all going with Si in his camper van. Sheeka can go with them and we'll all meet up in a day or two."

"Fine by me," says Chrissie airily, as though she doesn't have a care in the world.

I don't like the sound of this at all. I struggle to my feet, shaking myself. "No, no, no Chrissie," I whine. I can smell disaster. Don't go ahead with this plan. I plead with my eyes, but she's so busy talking about Brecon that I make no impression on her at all.

Dog-Dog's ears are up again. He knows I'm upset. "Don't be worried. I'm coming right behind you in a day or two. The hills are full of rabbits and there are lots of woods to roam about in. We'll be together all the time."

He licks me and I feel a bit comforted.

* * * * *

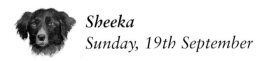

Sheeka
Sunday, 19th September

I'm in the back of Si's camper van, along with four little mutts and we set off in a procession of odd-looking, painted vehicles. At Salisbury, we branch off to deliver something to Si's mum and that's when my troubles begin.

The other dogs are all strangers to me. Lovelyboy, Crowbar and Custard wouldn't dream of behaving like this. This lot are young pups and have no respect for older folk. They chatter and bark all the time and they are not housetrained.

Si puts out bowls of food for us, and these cheeky pups push me aside and eat my share.

When I want to sleep one of them comes sniffing round me and says rude things about me.

"Give me a bit of peace!" I snap, exhausted by their restlessness.

"Ooooh!" squeaks one whippersnapper.

Another bares its milk teeth and growls in a very vulgar way.

I snap at them and they come for me.

"Pull her tail! Nip her paws! Scratch her ears!"

Never have I been so humiliated. How could Chrissie do this to me?

The noise is ugly, and Si stops the van. He yanks open the door to find out what's happening.

"Shurrup! Cut it out!" He has an unpleasant way. I can see why his dogs are just like him. One of the pups pees right next to where I'm sitting. That's the final straw. The next time we stop I'll make a run for it.

I should be with Chrissie and I'm going to find her. I'll travel to Brecon on my own. I'm not stupid; once I found my way from Henley all the way back home to Oxford.

When I feel the camper van stop I start barking. Si comes to the back and peers through the window. I move close to the door, getting ready. As he wrenches it open I leap out.

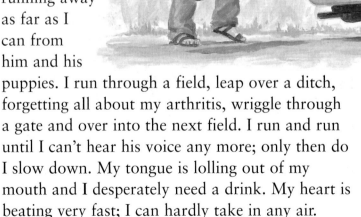

"Hey Sheeka! What's this? Come back, come here. *Heel!*"

But I am running away as far as I can from him and his puppies. I run through a field, leap over a ditch, forgetting all about my arthritis, wriggle through a gate and over into the next field. I run and run until I can't hear his voice any more; only then do I slow down. My tongue is lolling out of my mouth and I desperately need a drink. My heart is beating very fast; I can hardly take in any air.

"You silly old lady," I say to myself. "You're going to keel over. Find a drink." Luckily there's a cattle trough nearby and I lap up the lovely cold water till I'm about to burst. Then I look around me. The field is on top of a ridge, and way across the valley I can see the square tower of a church. Once I reach it I can find my bearings, and I'll be able to find my way to Brecon and my dearest Chrissie.

Suddenly there's a rumble of thunder. I haven't noticed that the afternoon has darkened. Blue lightning cracks the clouds. The heavens open and cold rain pours down. There isn't any shelter to be seen. I start trotting, out of one field and into another, on and on. The wind grows into a gale and the rain pelts down so I can hardly see. This

will be the death of me, I think. Oh Chrissie! Oh Dog-Dog! This is harder than I thought.

And then I am on a road; it's a small road, but a road that surely will lead to somewhere.

* * * * *

Pamela Norris
Sunday, 19th September

I don't enjoy matinée performances, because I always feel sleepy after lunch. Or else I find myself sitting next to a pensioner determined to munch through a whole box of chocolates. Today it was an entire tin of toffees. The crackle, crackle of the wrappers was driving me mad. The play was quite awful too, and I'm sure the leading lady was drunk.

I grabbed a quick coffee in Market Street and in my head I was already composing the review I was going to write for the Saturday paper. "This play was absolute rubbish from beginning to end. I was conscious for a moment at the beginning and fell into a deep slumber, only to wake up again right at the end ..."

No, I couldn't say that. How about, "A new play that combines the drama of EastEnders with the humour of Coronation Street, yet it left me in a state of rigid boredom ..."

Too rude. Oh dear, I'd better wait till I was sitting at my desk back home.

"Ho hum," I yawned widely, and soon I was in my little Mini driving past the square-towered cathedral, and heading for my bungalow and a pot of tea with a packet of chocolate biscuits.

The storm from the afternoon had died down and left a messy litter of broken branches and leaves on the road. I had an hour's drive ahead, and I didn't hurry because I was thinking of my review and what I would cook for supper. I took the minor road because it's such a nice drive home, but this evening all I could see was rain. I was peering ahead, puttering along, when I noticed a dog by the roadside. It was sitting on the verge, and as I approached it opened its mouth and barked at my car. I've never seen a dog behave in such a fashion, so I slowed down to look more closely.

After I'd gone past, and was about a hundred yards further on, I looked in my rear view mirror and it was still there, sitting by the verge, looking after the car. I slowed down, stopped and reversed. The dog and I stared with equal interest at one another for a few minutes. She barked again, a little aggrieved, as if to say, "This is me. If you don't like what you see, please look again." She was drenched to the skin, but there was a collar round her neck. I got out of the car. She stayed where she was, prim and well-mannered, paws neatly in front. Then she barked again, this time quite resentfully, I thought. The name on her collar was Sheeka.

"You're Sheeka," I said, "and I'm Pamela. Pamela Norris. You're lost, aren't you? Well, you'd better come with me and I'll take you to Wells police station. Let's see if they can find your owner. Hop in."

Chapter Four

Polly
Friday, 24th September

Before the crisis happened Polly had been
counting the days to their summer holiday. She
and Emilia were going to stay with Emilia's
mother, Nona, in Florence. Nona lived in a tall,
narrow, yellow-painted house with black, wrought
iron balconies. She kept white doves in the garden
and they clustered round the stone pond.

A fountain went drip,
drip, drip and Polly
could hear it at night.
Wasps settled on the
peaches in the tree
outside Polly's bedroom
and little wild
strawberries grew in

mossy corners. Polly loved going to Nona's, but they had put off their summer trip, hoping that Chrissie would soon come home. But that hadn't happened.

Dad was going to be away on a business trip to Chicago, but he made Emilia promise she and Polly would go away for a few days. "You both need a change, and you haven't seen Nona for nearly a year." Although he never mentioned Chrissie, Polly knew he was still angry with her.

But she could tell that he also felt sad and guilty about her. He had lost Chrissie's trust and didn't know how to get it back. One or two brief phone calls trickled in from Chrissie, but she never said exactly where she was. She clammed up totally about when she was coming home again, and if they ever tried to call her on her mobile phone it was switched off, or else just rang and rang. Chrissie, of course, was so angry with everyone and everything, that reaching her would have tried a saint's patience.

"I don't think she knows what she wants. Don't you remember being very confused at her age?" Emilia tried to explain, to try to soften Dad's anger.

"There's a limit to how much we can worry about Chrissie's future," he replied. "She's missed her A levels, so that's that. I just wish she would talk to me," he sighed. "At least we know she's all right and Sheeka's with her. We just have to leave her to work it out for herself. Really Emilia, she's got to face up to reality sooner or later. She'll be back when she runs out of money or grows up a little."

Both Emilia and Polly had gone through a phase of blaming themselves. "If only I'd shut up about Dizzy," thought Emilia. "If only I hadn't argued with her so much," thought Polly. Polly consoled herself that Chrissie had always managed to look after herself before – and besides, she still had Sheeka with her.

So Emilia went ahead and booked flights to Florence for them both. They couldn't wait for the day when they would leave Oxford and their worries behind. "It's still lovely and warm in Italy in September," promised Emilia.

* * * * *

Pamela Norris
Friday, 24th September

It's now the fifth day since my houseguest arrived. She's no trouble, but I can tell she's pining. The police said their kennels for lost dogs were full and they couldn't possibly take any more for the time being, so I had no choice but to bring her home.

She lies by the fire most mornings. It's turning out to be a dismal summer – damp and cold. Her paws cushion her face and she follows me about with her accusing eyes. I took her to the vet yesterday, because she hadn't touched any food since her arrival.

"She's healthy enough for her age," he said.

I noticed then that Sheeka pricked up her ears and looked at him sideways.

"I'd say she's about twelve or thirteen. Bit overweight, so it would be good for her to lose a few pounds. Boil a chicken and see if you can tempt her with some broth."

When he dismissed Sheeka with a pat on her rump, I could swear she looked offended. She did a little dancing side step, as though she were saying, "Watch your manners young man."

I'm getting used to having a dog around again after all these years. Good company when I write my nature articles and theatre reviews. She comes with me whenever I go out, and I've been reading all the notices about lost animals on trees and fences, in the hope that I might spot a description that fits her. One odd thing happened though. When we were in Taunton a few days ago, we passed a group of young people with their animals; they could have been travellers. Sheeka suddenly perked up. She whined and pulled at her leash and tried to get closer to them. Could it be that her owner is a traveller, too? Tomorrow I'll pin up descriptions of her around the area. But meanwhile we could tour around asking similar young people with dogs if they recognise Sheeka, or might know her owner.

* * * * *

Sheeka
Friday, 24th September

They say it happens suddenly, that one day you can't put two and two together, and that day has come. I've lost my sense of smell. I've never felt this way before, as though I don't know who I am.

I don't belong, that's what it is. I haven't seen Chrissie for such a long time now. I just can't bear it. I'm lost, unknown, in a strange country. Some days I can hardly bring myself to walk to the shops with Pamela.

She's kind, really kind, and I get chicken or beef every single day, and two walks. But she isn't the cuddly type and doesn't talk much. Even if I thump my tail to try and get her attention she won't look up from her book or computer. I miss Chrissie all the time. I miss Polly and Emilia almost as much. Pamela is a nice lady, but ...

Sometimes I go and sit by the gate and lift my

nose in the air to see if I can smell Chrissie coming. Nothing.

One day I saw some humans that looked like Chrissie's friends from the Glastonbury camp. They had big, heavy, mud-caked boots and dogs at heel.

Pamela's got sense; when I pulled at my lead, she immediately understood my interest. Now nearly all our walks are in the nearby towns, and we look for travellers with dogs. Pamela goes up and asks questions. "Have you heard of anyone who's lost their dog? Do you recognise Sheeka?" Even I manage to exchange some friendly words with my own kind.

Pamela has pinned notices with my photo on

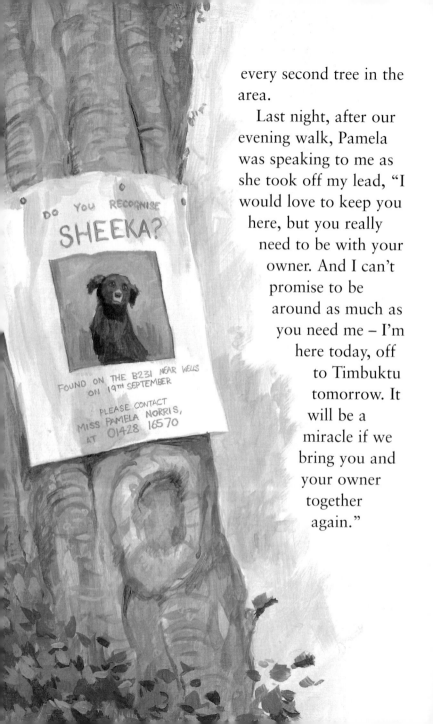

DO YOU RECOGNISE
SHEEKA?

FOUND ON THE B231 NEAR WELLS
ON 19TH SEPTEMBER

PLEASE CONTACT
MISS PAMELA NORRIS,
AT 01428 16570

every second tree in the area.

Last night, after our evening walk, Pamela was speaking to me as she took off my lead, "I would love to keep you here, but you really need to be with your owner. And I can't promise to be around as much as you need me – I'm here today, off to Timbuktu tomorrow. It will be a miracle if we bring you and your owner together again."

Chapter Five

Polly
Saturday, 25th September

The check-in time at Stansted Airport was two o'clock, which meant taking the nine o'clock bus from Oxford. At eight o'clock, in the middle of searching for Polly's sandals, the phone started ringing and Emilia answered it.

"Chreesie! How lovely to hear you darling. Are you all right? No! When was that? Oh, my goodness, I'm so sorry. But why didn't you tell us sooner?"

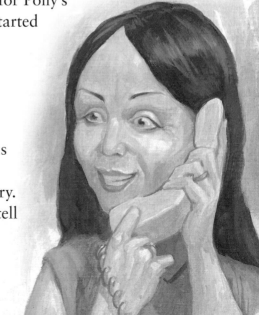

Her eyebrows shot up and there followed a long silence while Emilia listened intently. "Just a moment Chreesie." She cupped one hand over the receiver and signalled expressively with the other to Polly, who was hopping from one foot to the other, dying to know what had happened. "Sheeka has disappeared. Run away." She turned back to give Chrissie her attention again. "Sorry, but we are just now leaving to catch the bus for the airport. Yes, we'll be at Nona's. You've got her number, haven't you? Oh, my poor Chreesie, how terrible for you – also for us. You know how much we all adore Sheeka. Be strong, be positive – hope for a miracle and maybe Sheeka will find you soon. Bye for now, bye!"

On the journey and at the airport, Polly and Emilia were sunk in depression. Polly could take no pleasure in window shopping, or her hot chocolate and croissant, or the funny little shuttle train that took them to the place where they boarded the plane. She was so worried for Sheeka. Would Sheeka be able to survive on her own?

Sheeka was two years older than Polly; she'd been her loyal friend as long as she could remember. One of her favourite memories of Sheeka was the time Polly had been sent early to bed for being naughty. Sheeka had come upstairs into her room, looked with sympathy at the tear-stained face, jumped up on to the bed and kept Polly's legs warm. Later, when Dad looked in to say goodnight, Sheeka had growled threateningly at him.

"Don't you hurt my little girl," was the message. Dad had laughed and so had Polly. Sheeka was part of their lives. Polly thought she was just like Nana, the dog in *Peter Pan*. She understood situations, and she understood Polly and Chrissie.

Every school afternoon she waited for Polly and Chrissie by the front gate. Emilia said that Sheeka always stirred herself at 3.45 on the dot and ambled outside, rain or shine. But what would happen now? When Sheeka had been with Chrissie, she was like her guardian angel. But now that she'd disappeared how safe was Chrissie going to be? What would happen? Would Chrissie decide to come home again?

"Chrissie is very vulnerable," agreed Nona, talking about Chrissie over dinner that night. They ate melon, Parma ham and ravioli in the warm and fragrant garden. "She will go crazy without her

dog; truly crazy. Sheeka has to be found." Nona
had a decisive manner and great authority.

"I feel I should help look for Sheeka when we
get back," said Emilia.

"But what good will that do? The dog is lost,
gone somewhere and nobody
knows where. Sheeka doesn't
even know where she is
herself."

Nona remained silent
for a few minutes,
crumbling her bread
roll in her fingers.

"In such a
circumstance we
have to ask for a
miracle," she
finally said.

"A miracle?"
Polly frowned.
Miracles happened
in fairy tales, not in real life.
Maybe it was just Nona's way of saying that it
was hopeless. But Nona didn't mean that at all; in
fact, she meant the very opposite.

"We will make a trip to the town of Assisi and
we will ask Saint Francis to save Sheeka and

restore her to Chrissie, wherever she is. If anyone can find her, it will be Saint Francis. They say that when he was alive, more than 800 years ago, the birds used to fly down and listen to him. He is the patron saint of all animals. Anyway, I was hoping to take you both there to visit my cousin. It's only a few hours' drive away. So now we can ... not kill two birds with one stone – such an ugly thing to say – but feed two birds with one cake!"

* * * * *

Polly
Sunday, 26th September, 1.30 p.m.

After lunch Nona took Polly by the hand and led her to the dark little church next to the house. "Let's start by lighting a candle for Sheeka and Chrissie," she said.

Polly looked meaningfully at Emilia, who smiled back with a 'Let's humour Nona' nod. Polly was embarrassed at not knowing how to behave in an Italian church. She had a lot of questions about miracles and why Nona was so sure that Sheeka would be found if they prayed. Did Nona really believe that someone would shine a torch out of the sky and lead Sheeka back to

Chrissie and safety again? It was all so maddeningly
vague – a bit pointless and silly, she thought. Still,
she went off with Nona and lit a candle and sneezed
once or twice in the perfumed interior of the church.

After Nona had crossed herself with holy water

and they had come outside into the bright sunshine, she placed her hand kindly on Polly's head as though to say, "I know this is strange for you, but trust me."

Just before they set off for Assisi there was another phone call from Chrissie. Chrissie was sobbing as she spoke to Emilia. There was still no sign of Sheeka. She wanted to know when Emilia and Polly were coming back to England. "Suppose Sheeka turns up at home and there's no one to let her in?"

"I'll phone our neighbours to keep a look out. They'll feed her and take her in, Chreesie. Don't you worry," Emilia reassured her. "Now I have to go, we are on our way to Assisi with Nona today."

Chrissie seemed to have forgotten her former hostility to Emilia. Emilia was glad that at least some good had come out of the crisis. Polly was glad too, since she herself was very fond of Emilia, who was doing her best to be a good stepmother to the two girls.

"You know, Mama," said Emilia, "Chrissie is a dreamer; such an idealist. Her father can't understand that side of her at all. He can't see that his daughter is expressing something important. She's growing up and wants her father to take her seriously, even if they don't see eye to eye over everything. She wants him to listen to her, but he's so busy flying all over the world. He doesn't make enough time for her."

"Yes, I can see that," Nona said, thoughtfully. "There's something about her rebelliousness that reminds me of Saint Francis when he was a young man – he was just about her age too. He made his father very angry because he refused to follow his cloth-selling trade. His only wish was to be poor, like a beggar."

"Why, Nona?" Polly asked.

Nona had driven from Florence at breakneck speed, through Arezzo and Perugia, and they had almost arrived at their destination. "Because from a very young age Saint Francis realised that money and status were not important to him. Many holy people have understood that."

"So what did he do?"

"Gathered a group of men together, like himself, to pray, to help the sick and poor."

"And then what happened?"

"More and more people joined him. They are called Franciscans and now there are thousands of them all over the world. You'll see some in Assisi, dressed in brown robes and sandals."

* * * * *

Polly
Sunday, 26th September, 3.30 p.m.

Just before they arrived in Assisi, Nona pulled up in a lay-by and they got out to look at the view.

Polly saw a golden city perched on the hills, almost unreal in its beauty. Mount Subasio rose above gentle, green hills that provided a backdrop for the belfries and church domes of Assisi. In the foreground were splashes of misty red where poppies were blooming in the wheat fields.

"Isn't that magical?" Nona asked. "I love coming here, especially now I am an old

woman. But we are here on a pilgrimage, to ask
Saint Francis to bring Sheeka and Chrissie back
together again."

When they reached Assisi, Nona treated them
to coffee and ice cream in a café that overlooked a
busy piazza.

"My cousin Francesca has been a nun since the
age of twenty-six. She lives in a convent started by
a great friend of Saint Francis, Sister Clare.
Francesca is old now and not used to seeing a lot
of visitors, so today I will visit her by myself."

Emilia smiled. It was amusing to hear her mother on the subject of old people – after all, she herself was seventy-four, although it was hard to believe.

"I'm sure she will invite you for a cup of tea before we leave. But while I am with her, why don't you and Emilia look at the wall paintings in the Basilica. Sister Francesca and I will say a prayer for Chrissie and Sheeka, but Polly, you need to know from whom we're asking a favour."

Polly chewed her lip. She didn't want to be rude, but did Nona really think that saying prayers in Assisi could help Chrissie and Sheeka back home? Yet Polly was so worried that she would have tried anything. She would even pretend to believe in anything to bring her sister and Sheeka together again.

The ice cream was delicious. Polly wanted to lick the glass bowl. She quickly scoured the sides with her finger before anyone could stop her. The tip of her nose was flecked with white and Nona dabbed it gently with her lacy hankie.

"Isn't it crowded? Nearly as bad as Florence, but you notice the tourists more because it's so small," said Nona, gathering up her things. "They say Assisi is one of the holiest places in the world."

Little groups of young Italian men and women were strolling around; lines of tourists from all over the world clicked their cameras, and Polly felt the sunshine and festive atmosphere chasing away her sombre mood. There was something timeless about the cobbled lanes and old stone houses hung with red, trailing geraniums. She could almost believe that nothing much had changed in the last 800 years.

A boy of her own age was taking a cocker spaniel puppy for a walk. A feeling of great sadness came over Polly again. She'd always enjoyed taking Sheeka for walks. Chrissie had told her what an adorable puppy she'd been. Chrissie had smuggled Sheeka to school on several occasions. She'd kept the puppy in her satchel hanging over the back of her chair and somehow managed to keep her quiet during lessons. But one day the inevitable happened.

A small puddle appeared under Chrissie's chair, and both Chrissie and Sheeka had been sent home in disgrace.

Her daydream was abruptly shattered by the noise of a moped. It came roaring up one of the lanes leading to the open piazza and skidded to a noisy halt, nearly knocking down a Japanese couple who were nodding earnestly and consulting their guidebook. The teenager on the moped looked like a pop star, wearing wraparound shades and a red T-shirt. He glanced behind like a movie hero in a car chase, to check who was after him. Then, revving up his engine, he roared off again.

Emilia clicked her tongue impatiently. "I hope the police arrest him, silly show-off."

Polly thought he was rather wonderful.

"You know, Polly," Nona arranged some change on the table, "that's exactly how Saint Francis was as a young teenager: rich, reckless, and a show-off. There's hope for that young man on his flying moped! Right, *cara mia*, see you in about two hours. Bye!" Nona went off to meet her cousin.

Really, thought Polly, Nona was seeing Saint Francis in every other young person – first she'd compared Chrissie with him, now the boy on the scooter.

After the hot morning sun, the interior of the great church was like a cooling balm. Polly had to blink for a moment or two to get accustomed to the dim light. First, they looked at the tomb of Saint Francis, who was buried in the vaults, and then they admired the paintings in the lower part of the church, which was thronged with parties of reverent pilgrims led by a brown-robed nun or monk.

The upper church was enormous – high and wide and much lighter than the floor below. Every part of the walls and ceiling was painted in glorious colours with scenes from Saint Francis' life. Emilia took Polly's hand. "The paintings were done by a monk called Giotto. He was one of the first artists to want to paint real feeling and emotions in faces. Look, in this painting the young Saint Francis is feeling sorry for the poor beggar, so he gives him his own cloak. From his expression you can imagine the pity and love that makes him do that."

They passed slowly along the wall paintings admiring the different facial expressions – anger and sadness and happiness and greed and cunning – till they came to the painting that showed Saint Francis preaching to a flock of birds. Emilia put some coins in a box that activated a switch.

A brilliant white light flooded the picture.

Emilia bent down and said quietly, "I'm just going to the ladies. I'll be gone about five minutes. Can you wait here for me?"

Polly nodded, without taking her eyes off the face of the saint. There was nothing showy or colourful about the scene in the painting, but a tremendous calm strength seemed to come from the figure of Saint Francis bending over to talk to the birds clustered on the ground or fluttering in the air around him.

Without thinking what she was doing, Polly squeezed her eyes shut and wished hard for a miracle. "Let Sheeka be found, please," she muttered. "Please, please, please. Let Chrissie come home soon."

The thought flashed through her mind that Nona and her cousin were probably also saying their prayer for Sheeka and Chrissie. Were they kneeling on the floor, or had they gone to a chapel? When she opened her eyes the light had gone off, and she became aware of a strange vibration. It was hard to tell where it came from – it could have been from under her feet, but she felt it in her whole body. Incredibly, the floor felt as though it was gently rocking, like standing on the platform as a train was coming in. Then a low rumbling noise started to build up and the building seemed to tremble. People started to stir, like bees in a hive, and then they began screaming.

* * * * *

 Polly
Sunday, 26th September, 5.30 p.m.

An elderly American couple shouted, "Earthquake! Let's get outta here!"

Polly didn't know what to do. She stayed rooted to the spot. She felt paralysed. She couldn't see Emilia anywhere. She could taste fear in her mouth; it was like rusty metal on the back of her tongue.

Everyone was rushing to the exit as the rumbling

and tremors became stronger and stronger. The open doorway had become dark with figures jostling and pushing in their haste to get outside. Polly wanted to scream, but her throat was so dry that no sound came out. All of a sudden she felt someone grab her arm and hustle her in the direction of the front door. She gasped with astonishment: it was the young man she had seen on the moped, the one with the red T-shirt.

He was pushing her quickly, almost dragging her to safety when, with an almighty crash, the roof in the nave collapsed just metres from where Polly had been standing. She looked back to see clouds of dust and debris filling the church as though a bomb had exploded. Her mouth and nose

were filled with choking dust so she could hardly breathe.

"Presto, presto!" the young man cried frantically, dragging her out of the porch and into the open air. *"Mama? Mama?"* he demanded. A terrible noise echoed in the square: women wailing, babies crying, the hysterical sound of fire engines racing through the town and that awful, menacing rumble of the earth in angry protest.

But where was Emilia? Amid all the confusion Polly didn't see her. The young man was very agitated. He kept asking where her mother was. Then, at once, Emilia was there, swooping on Polly, hugging her tightly to herself. "Thank goodness you're safe! Come on, we must get away from these tall buildings." Then she remembered Polly's rescuer, and turned to thank him, but he had vanished. She clutched Polly's hand and Polly could feel her fear. "I've never known anything like this. Quick, come on, we must find Nona. We have to see if she's all right."

All around them crowds of tourists were pouring out of the Basilica. The air, earlier so lovely and fresh, was now full of swirling white dust.

Gasping for breath they ran up the hill towards Sister Francesca's convent as the ground continued to vibrate.

Chapter Six

Sheeka
Sunday, 26th September, 5.30 p.m.

One day, after I've been with Pamela for days and days, I wake up and feel terrible. I can't describe the feeling. It's like someone has put a clamp round my heart; that's how uncomfortable I feel. Maybe I'm going to have that heart attack that I've always feared. Oh well, there are worse ways to die. But first I want to see my Chrissie.

I get up and walk around. I drink a little water and nibble the chicken breast that Pamela has kindly given me from her own lunch. Nothing helps. My nostrils feel clogged and for some reason I can't explain, I lift up my head and bay. It is a vile noise.

"Dear oh dear, what a horrible racket! Something's been bothering you all morning, Sheeka. You're not ill are you?" A hand feels my nose. "Now come on," Pamela levels with me and looks deep into my eyes, "what are you thinking of?"

I wish I could tell. It *is* something, but I can't put a paw on it.

Pamela reaches up to the kitchen counter and switches on the six o'clock news. The announcer reads, "Assisi has been rocked by a severe earthquake. It measured 7.1 on the Richter scale. There has been large-scale damage to buildings. Priceless wall paintings of the life of Saint Francis have been almost destroyed. Several people are feared dead, including two

Franciscan monks who were examining the extent of the damage to the paintings inside the Basilica of Saint Francis. Some tourists were also hurt, but are now in a stable condition in the local hospital."

"What a tragedy!" Pamela declares. "Those lovely paintings. Imagine, they survived all of these 700 years and now they're a heap of rubble." She clicks her tongue sadly.

"Come on, Sheeka, what you need right now is a brisk walk. Blow away those cobwebs, shall we? Don't mope, there's a good dog."

She puts on her coat and hat and off we go again, in her yellow Mini, to see if we can find any clues about my owner.

* * * * *

Polly
Sunday, 26th September, 6.30 p.m.

Polly and Emilia were frantically hunting for Nona and Sister Francesca. Emilia looked like a wild woman. Her hair was in tangles and covered in dust and her face was streaked with dirt. The convent was undamaged, but Nona and her cousin were nowhere to be found.

"Really, I cannot understand why my mother

can't sit in one place. Why couldn't she be happy to sit and drink tea with Francesca here?"

Apparently the two old ladies had gone out for a stroll half an hour before the earthquake hit the town.

Polly and Emilia began by looking on the wooded hillside paths behind the convent and then, failing to find the two women, they went back into town. Nona's car was still parked in the central car park, although many of the visitors' cars had gone – driven off by frightened tourists.

The streets were packed with people, some staring at the cracks that had appeared in the walls of their houses, others standing around in a state of shock. Groups were hurriedly walking out of town to avoid the danger of more tremors. Several houses had collapsed.

Emilia held Polly's hand tightly as they walked quickly from one street to the next. Neither spoke, but both were hoping and praying that Nona and Francesca were safe.

Chapter Seven

Sheeka
Monday morning, 27th September

I don't know the exact time that it happened, but I find that I can breathe more easily again and notice that I'm taking in all the many interesting smells that had become a distant memory. The smell of flowering mustard mixed with fox; petrol fumes blended with rabbit; distant rain and fertiliser, and even the whiff of fish brought in by some seagull. I feel better, so much fitter and stronger than I've been for ages. Sitting up in the back seat, where Pamela has thoughtfully provided me with a warm rug, I start to take an interest in the passing landscape. Suddenly, I'm sure everything will turn out well.

We bowl along for about an hour and then Pamela slows down to turn into a lay-by.

"What's that funny noise in the engine?" she mutters to herself. She opens the rear door for me to stretch myself while she looks under the bonnet.

I walk slowly up to a gate that leads into a field. There's something I recognise in this place, something familiar, which signals that I've been there before. Sniffing intently around an oak tree over-shadowing the gate, I can just make out a memory of dog. Now what does that remind me of? Suddenly I remember. That's it! Those darned puppies at the back of Si's camper. No wonder this place is so familiar! This was where Si stopped. I remember the moment I jumped out and started running. First, I'd wriggled through the gate, then I'd dashed across the field of cabbages and then on and on and on, goodness knew through how many fields and woods and ditches. Then the thunderstorm had come, and finally I'd hit a road and stopped on the verge, miserable and drenched to the skin, which is when Pamela had rescued me. I circle the tree with great excitement, reliving the past.

Pamela is leaning on the gate when I look up to thank her. Without her shelter I'd be dead by now, for sure. I whine to get her attention and lick her hand.

She pats me absent-mindedly, gazing out over the cabbages, blue-grey in colour with small white butterflies dancing over them in the setting sun.

She turns to me. "I don't know, Sheeka, I just don't know. I think you might have to get used to the idea of living with me from now on. We've done our best. I'll give the animal charities another call tomorrow, but there's not a huge amount more I can do. Think you can put up with me, do you? I know I'll be second best, but there's no other solution."

I sigh, so sorry for her feelings of disappointment. Deep inside me, though, I have a strong instinct that this isn't the end of the story.

Something more is definitely going on. A lark trills high up in the sky, a breeze shakes the leaves on the oak and moves on west. A flock of pigeons land on the cabbage field a little way off from the gate. They are a darker grey than the cabbages, and stare at me with beady eyes.

"Come on," Pamela says briskly, "we must get some petrol," and we move off again, leaving the field and the gate and the oak tree behind us.

In a little while, the bright red signs of a petrol station appear in front of us. The smell of petrol overpowers everything, but I catch a familiar scent. For no reason that I can understand, my heart suddenly starts to beat with the most uncontrollable excitement. Boom-boom, boom-boom. What is going on?

Pamela draws up on the forecourt and opens her door. To my own astonishment I start to bark and bark. It's uncontrollable. I can't stop myself.

Pamela holds up a warning finger. "Sheeka! Stop it!"

But my barking is a reflex reaction. Why? There's only one car in front of us whose driver is just returning, after paying for his petrol, slipping his wallet back into his pocket. I certainly don't know him, although he looks a bit like a traveller with his heavy boots and untidy, rough sweater.

I can't see the passenger in front and the forecourt is otherwise deserted. So what has set my alarm bells ringing?

My barking is so loud that the man looks at me jumping around on the back seat, making an infernal racket. He peers inside the window of his own car to say something to the passenger. Then he gets in, starts the engine and drives off.

Pamela is on her way back to the car after paying when she stops to pick up something – the man's wallet, which has fallen out of his pocket. Pamela runs out into the road waving it and shouting, but the other car is too far away by now.

Quickly she jumps into our car and follows him, flashing her lights and honking the horn. The man who has lost his wallet must have realised she is chasing him, because he finally does slow down and pulls up by the roadside. Looking a little annoyed, he walks over to see what the fuss is about. The second person in the car also opens the passenger door and I find myself barking uncontrollably again. But as soon as this other person emerges from the car, everything makes sense. The whole world is mended and all the hurts and sorrows disappear in an instant, because there, coming towards me, is my beloved Chrissie!

How shall I describe our meeting? Her mouth has fallen open, her eyes are wide and wonder-struck, a smile as big as the sun lights her face.

"SHEEKA!"

What joy, what confusion, what tears, what happiness, what celebration!

"Oh Sheeka, you're okay! I've missed you so much; I've been so worried!

I've been wandering around for weeks, just looking everywhere, hoping someone would have heard about you or given you shelter. My friend Dave's been helping – we've driven all over looking for you," she explains, hugging me tight.

Pamela is grinning from ear to ear. "What a miracle!" she declares. "Out of all the petrol stations in the country!"

"And if I hadn't dropped my wallet, you wouldn't have come after us," said Dave.

"And if Sheeka hadn't known something she wouldn't have barked like she did. You did say something to me about a crazy dog barking, didn't you, Dave?" Chrissie says, nearly strangling me in a bear hug.

"You must both come home with me and let's have some tea together to celebrate," says Pamela, generously. She leans inside to switch off the radio, when suddenly Chrissie lets go of me, shouting, "No! Leave it."

It's the latest update on the news about the Assisi earthquake.

"My sister and stepmother are there," she says, and bursts into tears.

* * * * *

Sheeka
Monday evening, 27th September

When we get back to Pamela's bungalow, Chrissie tries to make contact with Emilia and Polly. "I can't get an answer from Emilia's mobile," says Chrissie.

"Maybe her batteries have run down," suggests Pamela, putting on the kettle.

"Call your father," Dave suggests.

"But I can't."

"Oh come on, Chrissie. Just ring him."

So reluctantly, Chrissie does. A wave of relief passes over Chrissie's face as she hears the good news. "Polly and Emilia are safe and so is Nona. Her cousin, Francesca, fell and cut her leg, but it isn't too serious. They're flying back to England today. Dad was really nice. I'm going to go home tomorow and see them."

Pamela offers to drive Chrissie and me back home to Oxford the next day. Dave says he has to get back to the camp.

"Will you be okay, Chrissie?"

"I'll be fine. Thanks for everything. Give lots of love to Scarlett and Id and Dog-Dog. Thank everyone in the camp for being family to me."

* * * * *

Sheeka
Tuesday, 28th September

On the long drive home Chrissie and Pamela talk all the way – they seem to really like one another. They have a lot in common – the theatre, and travelling – and me. By the time they arrive in Oxford they have become firm friends.

"If you like, you can come and stay with me for a while," Pamela says to Chrissie. "You'll be able to come with me to plays – I always get two tickets. And if you decide to do your A levels again, I can help you. I'm a retired teacher. I'm sure you could get the grades you need to get into drama school."

"What do you think, Sheeka?" Chrissie asked.

I thump my tail in approval. It sounds like a very good idea.

"Brilliant," says Chrissie. "But first I have to get back to my family and make sure they're all right."

I think about the events of the day before and feel happy again. From despair to happiness, from gloom to rejoicing! Chrissie leans round and strokes my head. I think she feels the same way, too.

* * * * *

Polly
Tuesday, 28th September

Chrissie and Sheeka were home in Oxford by ten o'clock and Polly, Emilia and Dad were waiting to welcome the runaways and Pamela with hot chocolate and Sheeka's favourite biscuits. Dad put his hand on Chrissie's shoulder. "Darling, I've missed you. I'm so glad you're home. Let's see if we can work things out together."

"It feels good to be home, Dad."

"Oh Sheeka, we missed you too," said Dad, trying to hug Chrissie and Sheeka at the same time.

"Emilia, I've been sick with worry about you and Polly ever since I heard about the earthquake. What were you doing in Assisi?" Chrissie demanded.

"Well," said Polly, "it's hard to explain, but it's like this. Nona took us there because she said that Saint Francis would rescue Sheeka – he's the patron saint of animals, in case you didn't know – and somehow you and Sheeka found each other the very next day!"

"Goodness!" exclaimed Pamela. "It does seem miraculous."

"How do you explain it?" Chrissie asked.

Polly hopped from one foot to the other. "Well, Nona says it's a miracle."

Dad looked uncomfortable. "A coincidence, maybe?"

Polly said, "If it is, it's an unbelievably huge, enormous coincidence."

"Then it must be a miracle," declared Chrissie.

Whether it was a miracle or not, Sheeka just couldn't stop wagging her tail.